בס"ד

This book belongs to:

לה׳ הארץ ומלואה

Please read it to me!

Hachai

Perfect Porridge

A Story About Kindness

by Rochel Sandman

illustrated by
Chana Zakashansky-Zverev

In memory of
Zayde Mendel & Bubbe Hinda.
who set a shinning example for all their descendents.

Dedicated By
Dovid Shlomo & Sara Deitsch

Mordecai & Brana Shaina Deitsch & Family
Joseph & Shterna Deitsch & Family
Rochel Leah & Yosef Tzvi Sandman & Family
Ella & Mayer Zeiler & Family
Chanah Devorah & Yankel Pinson & Family

Zalman Deitsch, Avrohom Moshe Deitsch,
Yosef Deitsch & Gavriel Gopin

Rivkin, Gorowitz, Brook & Karp Families

★★★

Perfect Porridge

*With love and thanks to my parents, Dovid and Sara Deitsch,
who learned from and carried further the goodness and generosity
of Bubbe Hinda and Zayde Mendel. R.S.*

*To my heroic grandfather, Roman Isaakovich Goldshmidt, who fought
against the Nazis and to my grandmother, Keyla Goldshmidt, who survived
the hardships of war in Uzbekistan just like the characters in this book. C.Z.*

★★★

First Edition - March 2000 / Adar II 5760
Second Impression - March 2003 / Adar II 5763

Editor: Devorah Leah Rosenfeld

LCCN: 99-65449
ISBN: 0-922613-92-3

HACHAI PUBLISHING
Brooklyn, N.Y. 11218
Tel: 718-633-0100 - Fax: 718-633-0103
www.hachai.com - info@hachai.com

Printed in China

Bubbe Hinda and Zayde Mendel left their home carrying just
a few precious things. Bubbe Hinda took her Shabbos candlesticks
and her big iron pot so she could make porridge.

Zayde Mendel took his tefillin, his tallis and a few holy books
so he'd be able to learn Torah.

Their new home was tiny and bare, but at least it was far away from the War.

Bubbe missed her old neighbors and friends. Zayde missed having a study partner to learn with and students to teach.

Yet Bubbe Hinda and Zayde Mendel were thankful to Hashem. They were safe. They had their health. And they had some food to eat.

"Not everyone has as much as we have," said Zayde Mendel. "How can we help the sick and the hungry people who have come here to escape the War?"

"I know!" said Bubbe Hinda.

Her eyes were shining as she told Zayde Mendel her idea.

"I will go to the breadline each day and collect a bit of bread from everyone in the line. Then I will go and feed those bits of bread to the sick. After that, I will come home and cook porridge for the hungry people I meet in the market."

Zayde Mendel shook his head.

"A wonderful plan, Hinda, but it is too much for one person. Since you speak the language better than I do, you can collect the bread in the market. Then you can go to feed the sick people.

"I will stay here and cook the porridge. When you meet hungry people in the market, just bring them home to me."

Bubbe Hinda looked surprised.
"But Mendel," she said, "you don't
have time. You learn Torah all day."

"So," answered Zayde,
"I'll learn Torah at night."

"But Mendel," she said, "you don't
know how to cook!"

"True," answered Zayde,
"but I've seen you cook
a thousand times.
How hard could it be?"

The next day,
Bubbe Hinda
gave Zayde
Mendel the
grain for
the porridge.

"Are you sure you don't want me to cook it?" she asked.

"The sick people are waiting for their bread, Hinda. You go. I'll be fine." Zayde Mendel smiled and waved as Bubbe Hinda went off to the market carrying an empty sack. Bubbe Hinda smiled and waved back.

After davening, Zayde Mendel set to work. He lit the fire. He went to the well and got a few pails of water. He filled the pot with water, poured in the grain, and sat down to learn. The water and the grain cooked and bubbled. Zayde Mendel smiled as the smell of porridge filled the house.

Late that afternoon, Bubbe Hinda arrived with a few hungry
people.

She leaned over the pot and stuck a long wooden spoon
inside. As Bubbe lifted the spoon for a taste, she saw a tiny
black pebble in the spoon!

"Mendel," she whispered, "did you check the grain?"

"No," answered Zayde Mendel. "Why?"

Bubbe Hinda held out the spoon with the pebble.
"Whenever you cook porridge, you must first check the grain and
take out the grass, pebbles, and anything else that doesn't
belong. Then you must wash the grain to remove the dirt
that's left."

"Oh," said Zayde Mendel. He was very quiet.

"Don't worry," said Bubbe Hinda. "It won't go to waste! You
go learn."

Bubbe Hinda took the big pot in her strong arms and emptied it outside near the neighbor's cow.

Zayde Mendel watched as the cow ate all of the dirty porridge. Then he sat down at the table with the hungry guests and began learning Torah. Soon everyone was learning with him.

Bubbe Hinda toasted some bread and made some tea.
The hungry people washed their hands and said a brocha.
They ate the little meal and then thanked Hashem.

The next day when Bubbe Hinda went off to the market, she waved to Zayde Mendel and called out, "Don't forget to check the grain."

"Check the grain," Zayde Mendel said to himself.
"How hard could it be?"

Zayde Mendel went to the well and brought back a few pails of water. He filled the pot with water and hung it on a hook.

Then he checked the grain near the sunny window. He took out all the bits of grass. He took out all the tiny pebbles. He rinsed it carefully with water, poured it into the pot, and sat down to learn.

Late in the day, Bubbe Hinda arrived with a few more hungry people.

She sniffed the air, but the house didn't smell like porridge. She leaned over the pot and saw some very clean grain sitting in some very cold water.

"Mendel," she whispered, "I see you checked the grain, but you forgot to light the fire!"

"Oh," said Zayde Mendel. He looked at the floor.

"Don't worry," said Bubbe Hinda. "It won't go to waste! You go learn."

Zayde Mendel sat down at the table with the hungry guests and began learning Torah. Soon everyone was learning with him.

Bubbe Hinda quickly lit the fire, and before long the porridge was ready.

The hungry people said a brocha and ate, then thanked Hashem when they were full.

The next day when Bubbe Hinda went off to the market, she waved to Zayde Mendel and called out, "Don't forget to light the fire. Don't forget to check the grain."

"Light the fire. Check the grain," Zayde Mendel said to himself. "How hard could it be?"

After davening, Zayde Mendel lit the fire. He went to the well and got a few pails of water. He filled the pot with water, checked and washed the grain, and poured it into the pot.

Then, with a tired sigh, Zayde Mendel sat down to learn.

The porridge cooked and bubbled all day, and soon the tiny house smelled wonderful.

That afternoon, Bubbe Hinda arrived with a whole group of hungry people. She leaned over the pot, stuck a long wooden spoon inside, but no porridge came out. It was all stuck to the bottom of the pot in one big lump!

"Mendel," she whispered, "I see you
 lit the fire and checked the grain,
 but did you stir the porridge?"

"No," answered Zayde Mendel.
"Why?"

"Unless you stir the porridge,
 it sticks to the pot like glue."

"Oh," said Zayde Mendel.

"Don't worry," said Bubbe Hinda.
"It won't go to waste! You go learn."

Zayde Mendel sat down at the table with their hungry guests and began learning Torah. Soon everyone was learning with him.

Bubbe Hinda quickly scraped the lumpy porridge out of the pot and cut it into slices. She added salt and fried each slice in some oil.

Bubbe Hinda served the first portion to Zayde Mendel, who looked closely at the new food.

"Porridge latkes?"
he asked.

Bubbe Hinda
smiled at him.
"I told you
it wouldn't
go to waste."

The hungry people
said a brocha and ate,
then thanked Hashem
when they were full.
Not a single porridge
latke was left.

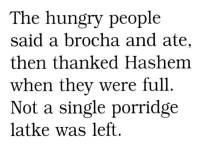

The next day when Bubbe Hinda went off to the market, she waved to Zayde Mendel and called out, "Don't forget to light the fire! Don't forget to check the grain! Don't forget to stir the porridge!"

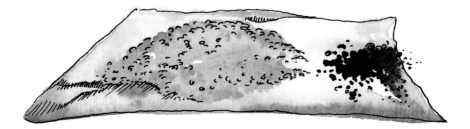

"Light fire, check grain, stir porridge," Zayde Mendel said to himself.

"Light fire, check grain, stir porridge," he repeated as he brought the water from the well. "Light fire, check grain, stir porridge," he sang as he poured the water into the pot and hung it on the hook. All that morning, the fire danced, the clean grain bubbled and Zayde Mendel stirred.

When Bubbe Hinda came home, a parade of hungry people followed her right up to the door. She leaned over the pot, stuck a long wooden spoon inside, and took out a tiny bit of porridge. She sniffed it. She blew on it. She said a brocha and took a little taste. She closed her eyes and swallowed.

Bubbe Hinda looked right at Zayde Mendel and said, "This porridge is perfect . . . better than mine!"

Zayde Mendel stood a little straighter
and smiled at his wife.

"To make perfect porridge," he said,
"is harder than it looks!"

The hungry people said a brocha and ate, then thanked Hashem when they were full.

They all stayed and learned Torah late into the night.

From then on, Bubbe Hinda had new neighbors and friends. Zayde Mendel had study partners to learn with and students to teach.

"A good deed is like making perfect porridge," Zayde Mendel always told them. "You have to take the time to do it right."